THE JUNIOR
NOVELIZATION

THE JUNIOR NOVELIZATION

By Ellen Weiss

**Adapted from the screenplay
written by Jerry Juhl and Joseph Mazzarino
and Ken Kaufman**

MUPPET PRESS
Grosset & Dunlap • New York

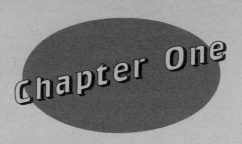

Chapter One

*I*t was a dark and stormy night. *Very* dark. *Very* stormy. Lightning forked across the lowering sky, and thunder rumbled ominously, shaking the ark that Noah had built to save the animals from the coming flood.

Noah watched them file onto the boat, two by two. He nodded in satisfaction: It was done. All the animals were safe on the ark. He stepped aboard and prepared to shut the door.

But wait—what was that noise? Could it be a last-minute straggler?

"No! Wait!" screamed a high, cracking voice. Noah peered out into the rain to see who it was. "Don't leave without me!" yelled the voice.

A figure stumbled out of the darkness and fell into Noah's arms, gasping for air. It wore a muddy woolen robe, and had a large blue beaky sort of thing for a nose. It was Gonzo the Great.

"Please, Mr. Noah, I want to come with you," Gonzo begged breathlessly.

Noah eyed him suspiciously. "You're alone," he remarked.

Gonzo's face was lit by a terrifying flash of lightning. "No, no. My friends are here somewhere," he said. He craned his neck to get a view through the doorway of the ark. There, just inside, he could see them all. "There's Kermit, and Piggy! Hey, Rizzo!" he called to them.

Noah was not convinced. "You're not a frog or a pig or a rat," he said. "What are you, anyway?"

There was a great clap of thunder, and a flash of lightning that illuminated the pain on Gonzo's face. He had heard this question before, and he had never found the answer.

"I'm a...you know..." he trailed off, shrugging. "Whatever."

"What do you mean?" demanded Noah. "What is your species?"

"I guess there's only one of me," Gonzo responded limply.

"Then you are doomed!" Noah's voice was as loud as the thunder.

As Noah slammed the door in his face with a resounding *boom*, Gonzo took one last desperate look at Kermit and the others. He was crushed.

And then, a miracle! The door opened again!

Gonzo looked up, full of hope, to see Noah's arm shoot out. It was holding a very small umbrella.

"Oh. You may need this," said Noah. He handed the umbrella to Gonzo and slammed the door once more.

As if on cue, the rain began to come down in torrents. "Wait! Don't leave me!" Gonzo howled. "*Noooooooo!!!*"

• • •

"*Noooooooo!!!*"

In the room he shared with Rizzo at the Muppet boarding house, Gonzo tossed and shouted in his bed. Rizzo snored away in the hammock above him. Holding his pillow over his head like an umbrella, Gonzo sat bolt upright. He knocked his head on Rizzo's hammock and sent his little rodent friend flying.

"*Ahhhh!*" shrieked Rizzo.

"I don't want to be alone!" wailed Gonzo.

"You're not alone," said a voice.

"Who said that?" Gonzo was mystified.

"Gee, let me see. Could it be the rat hanging out the window?"

Gonzo jumped up and looked out the window, where he found Rizzo hanging precariously from the sill.

"Sorry, buddy. I had that weird dream again," Gonzo said, pulling him back inside.

"The one with the goat, the midget, and the jar of peanut butter?" Rizzo asked.

"No, no. The one where. . . Nah, forget it. You wouldn't understand."

"I'd understand," said Rizzo. "Come on, we're roommates. I'm here for you, man."

"Okay. Well, I'm talking to this Noah guy who won't let me on his boat because I'm . . ." Gonzo began.

He was interrupted by a loud snore. Rizzo was fast asleep.

". . . alone," Gonzo finished. "Good night, Rizzo." He sighed and turned back to the window, staring up at the starry sky. A bright object streaked across the heavens. "Whoa," said Gonzo.

● ● ●

The rosy glow of the sun's first rays lit up the Muppet boarding house, complete with its peeling paint and crooked shutters. It might have been falling apart, but it was home. Behind the wash that hung in the front yard, the Electric Mayhem band's bus sat rusting quietly in the driveway.

Alarm clocks began going off all over the house. Hands—green ones, blue ones, pink ones, furry ones—reached out to shut them off.

In his room, Kermit slid out of bed, stretched, and yawned. Ambling through the door, he pulled it shut behind him. The doorknob came off in his hand.

No sooner had Kermit stepped out of his room than he was nearly knocked over by a procession of weird characters storming down the hallway. "Sheesh!" said Kermit. Pepe, a towel around his waist (if a shrimp actually *has* a waist) brought up the rear. Kermit followed him down the hall. There was already a line for the bathroom, though nobody really seemed to mind. Ahead of Kermit, Janice worked on her yoga. Animal was cutting to the head of the line while brushing his teeth.

Inside the bathroom, the usual morning madness prevailed. The Electric Mayhem band gathered around the mirror, doing their thing. Floyd waxed his moustache. Zoot brushed his sax. Animal spit his toothpaste into the sax, and Zoot shot him a look. Dr. Teeth buffed his shiny gold tooth with a big car-wax buffer.

Fozzie came out of the shower wearing a raincoat and rain hat, and Animal got in. Meanwhile, Pepe showered in the sink, while several penguins slid into a bubble bath. Animal got out of the shower. And just as it was finally Kermit's turn to bathe, Animal turned on his giant hair dryer full blast, practically blowing Kermit right back out the bathroom door.

Elsewhere in the house, Rizzo, straining and groaning, was doing sit-ups with his Ab-Isolator—fashioned from a big mousetrap. Tacked to the ceiling directly above him was a pin-up poster of the

"Mice Girls." "I do it all for you, ladies!" he said to the picture. As if in answer, the mousetrap snapped shut, folding Rizzo neatly in half.

It was time for breakfast. The main dining room was beginning to fill up. Pepe, an apron tied around his, er, waist, rushed around with plates of food. As Sweetums walked down the stairs, Andy and Randy Pig slid down the railing and sailed off, landing in front of Sam the Eagle, who was dressed in an American flag gym outfit. Sam was barking out exercise positions to a roomful of confused chickens.

Meanwhile, Clifford was on the phone with his girlfriend. The phone cord was stretched across the kitchen doorway. "Baby, don't be mad, you know I love you!" Clifford wheedled. "Can you hold on a second?" He hit the call-waiting button. "Hey, sweet thing," he said to caller number two. "I was just thinkin' about you too...."

Kermit ducked under the phone cord, went into the kitchen, and grabbed some juice. At the kitchen counter, the Swedish Chef was making pound cake— or at least he was pounding repeatedly on a cake.

"Nu krustra brekkie fuddnna pounda cake!" said the Swedish Chef with enthusiasm.

Back in the dining room, Kermit sat down at the breakfast table, joining Fozzie, Scooter, Rowlf, and a crowd of others. They ate fast as they read the paper and prepared for their busy days. Breakfast time at the Muppet boarding house was like rush hour at Grand Central Station. It was the one time of day when everybody in this wacky family touched base with everybody else.

This morning, Fozzie was trying out some new jokes. "Okay. Two peanuts are walking down the street, and one was assaulted. Get it? A-salted? Ahh*aaa*!"

Nobody laughed.

Kermit lowered his newspaper. "Audition, Fozzie?" he asked.

"Yeah. What do you think?" Fozzie wanted to know.

"Faster," was Kermit's recommendation. "And funnier."

"Thanks, Kermit!"

Suddenly, Miss Piggy burst into the room. "Good morning, everyone!" she gushed. "What an absolutely splendid day."

"Good morning, Piggy. How are you?" said Kermit.

"Late," replied Miss Piggy. "I start my fabulous new job today. We megastar TV journalists have to be punctual, you know."

"TV journalist?" said Kermit quizzically. "When did you…?"

Miss Piggy snatched a doughnut off a plate and beat a hasty retreat. "Gotta run! Ta-ta, my sweet!" She blew a kiss on her way out the door.

Kermit went back to reading his paper. He looked up when Pepe came out of the kitchen.

"Kermit," said Pepe, "you fix the oven yet?"

Kermit frowned. "What's wrong with...?"

An explosion rocked the kitchen, and the oven door flew into the dining room, followed by large amounts of smoke.

The Swedish Chef appeared in the doorway, coughing. "Hudy hundy ovena broke a hu!"

Kermit sighed. "I'll put it at the top of my list," he said.

The next time Kermit looked up from the news of the day, the others were gone. Gonzo, still in his pajamas and robe, had finally drifted downstairs. He moved slowly through the room, absorbed in thought, and sat down at the table next to Kermit.

"Hey, Gonzo, aren't you supposed to perform at that bar mitzvah today?" Kermit asked him.

"Nah," replied Gonzo. "The Electric Mayhem's covering for me." He sighed heavily.

"But you never miss the chance to shoot yourself out of a cannon," Kermit said to him, perplexed. "What's wrong?"

"Nothing. I guess I'm just tired of being a one-of-a-kind freak."

"Gonzo, you're not a one-of-a-kind freak, you're, you're . . ." Kermit trailed off, unable to find the right words.

"A whatever?" said Gonzo helpfully.

"Well…ummm…" said Kermit.

"See? I mean, I don't even know where I come from. My earliest memory is knocking on this red door and you saying, 'Come on in!'"

Kermit smiled. "Well, you did have one heck of a tire-eating act!"

Gonzo was flattered by the compliment. "Yeah, you know, I did!"

They both chuckled at the memory. Just then Clifford popped his head in the door. "Yo, Kerm!" he said. "You weren't waiting on some house painters, were you?"

"Yes…" Kermit said.

"Well, they're just driving away," Clifford informed him. "Animal bit one of them."

"What? Don't let them go!" Kermit yelled. He ran outside, waving his arms in desperation. Then, a second later, he reappeared.

"You know what you are, Gonzo?" Kermit said.

"What?" said Gonzo.

"*Distinct*," said Kermit. And then he was gone again, shouting after the painters: "Wait, fellas! He didn't mean it! He's just a musician!"

Gonzo, finally alone in the quiet house, sighed. He looked at the photographs on the hutch beside him. Kermit and Robin. Miss Piggy with her nephews. Fozzie with his mother. Rizzo and his huge rat family.

And there was another photo, a long, long shot of a lone little speck in the middle of the desert. That was Gonzo, all by himself.

"Distinct, huh? More like *extinct*," he muttered.

Oh, well. It was time for breakfast. He picked up the box of Kap'n Alphabet cereal sitting on the table beside him. On the front of the box was a picture of a really dumb-looking sea captain. Gonzo poured the cereal into the bowl, but some of it spilled out onto the table. "Oops," he said.

Gonzo started to sweep the spilled cereal off the table, but suddenly stopped. The letters were re-arranging themselves, spelling something.

R U THERE?

Gonzo stared at the letters for a moment, speechless with amazement. Then he jumped out of his seat.

"Wow! Somebody! Hey!" he yelled.

Rizzo came into the dining room.

"I think my Kap'n Alphabet is sending me a message!" shouted Gonzo.

"I know what you mean," Rizzo responded. "Last night I had some guacamole, and it's still talkin' to me."

"Look! I'm not kidding!"

Rizzo peered at the spilled cereal. He gave Gonzo a quizzical look. There was no message. It had disappeared, leaving a random pile of letters.

"But—it was here just a second ago!" Gonzo protested in confusion. "It said 'Are you there?'"

"Are you sure it didn't say 'Are you nuts?'?"

Gonzo frantically blew and poked at the cereal as Rizzo eyed him suspiciously. "Uh," said Rizzo at last, "maybe you and the Kap'n would like to be alone." He returned to the kitchen, shaking his head.

Gonzo was not about to give up on his talking cereal, however. He turned the box over and shook it, spilling more cereal and a toy telescope onto the table.

"Hmmm," Gonzo said. "A telescope. Cool."

The cereal letters started moving again. This time they spelled out:

WATCH THE SKY

"Watch the sky! Whoa!" cried Gonzo. He grabbed the toy telescope and headed to the boarding house roof to do just that.

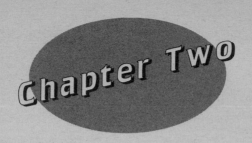

Chapter Two

At that moment, a cement truck was pulling up outside a lone industrial-looking building in the middle of nowhere—or at least a part of town that wasn't any fun to hang around in. The truck rolled toward the twelve-foot-high chain-link fence topped by coils of razor wire, stopped at the guardhouse, and continued through the gate. A sign above the gate read AAA CEMENT COMPANY. A security camera hidden in the sign stayed trained on the truck as it entered the building.

This was no cement factory.

Inside the building, a set of elevator doors opened, and a sour-looking military officer, wearing a lot of medals, stepped off. He was met by Rentro, a friendly but slow-moving bear.

"Good morning, sir," said Rentro, and then led the way down a long, curved hallway until they reached an intersection, at which point the bear seemed a bit lost. "Um . . . It would be—this way, sir," Rentro said, not looking too sure.

They finally reached their destination, a small chamber in front of an official-looking door. On the wall beside the door was an electronic gadget, just at Rentro's eye level.

"New retinal scanner," Rentro explained. "For security." Then he put his face to the scanner, pressed a button, and was immediately blinded by a flash of light. Rentro stepped back, momentarily sightless and disoriented. "Gotta love that," he said, shaking his head.

The door whooshed open. "We can go in now," said Rentro. He bashed blindly into the man, who was already entering.

On the other side of the door was a large, imposing office, furnished with a large, imposing desk. Behind the desk was a high-backed chair, turned away from the door.

"General Luft, sir," Rentro said, announcing the visitor to the occupant of the chair. The chair spun around quickly to reveal Rentro's boss, an intense-looking man named K. Edgar Singer. Rentro turned and left the room.

"Ah, General Luft," said Singer. "Welcome to Covnet."

"I'm on a schedule, Singer," snapped the general. "What have you got?"

"Evidence, sir. Hard evidence." Singer stalled, searching for something on his desk. Then he leaned into the intercom. "Rentro! The remote!" he barked to his assistant.

At his station outside the door, Rentro was just about to eat his favorite lunch, a sticky fluffer-nutter sandwich. "Yes, sir," he replied into the intercom. He picked up the remote with hands that were completely gooey with peanut butter and marshmallow.

Inside the office, Singer was explaining things to the general. "Over the last few months," he said, "we've intercepted some communications not of this Earth." When he saw Rentro entering with the remote, he stretched out his hand for it. Rentro placed the sticky remote in Singer's hand, and Singer glared at Rentro.

Rentro leaned toward Luft. "Alien slime, sir," he said. "It's everywhere."

Singer aimed the remote at the paneled wall that hid the TV screen. The panels immediately began to go wild, opening and closing like mad. Singer sighed.

"Bottom button, sir," Rentro suggested helpfully.

Again, Singer pushed a button on the remote. This time the lights in the room went out.

Rentro cleared his throat. "Bottom right, sir."

The lights came back on, then dimmed gradually as the big TV screen lit up. On it was a photograph of the Great Wall of China. But something about this picture was not right—something about the stones. Some of them were protruding from the wall to form a pattern. They spelled out a message: R U THERE?

"This same message, 'Are you there?', has appeared all around the world," Singer reported to the general. "These are the instances we were lucky enough to capture on film." He clicked the remote and the next image came up: an Egyptian pyramid with R U THERE? carved into it.

Singer kept clicking. He showed Luft a photo of Stonehenge, in which the stone pillars formed the giant letters R U THERE? Next there was an image of the HOLLYWOOD sign. It spelled out R U THREE?

"I know this one says 'Are you three?' but we believe it to be a simple spelling error," said Singer.

"But this could be vandalism, a practical joke!" spluttered Luft.

"See, now that's what I said," Rentro said. Singer just glared at him.

The next thing Singer displayed on the screen was a map of the U.S. with a spiral overlaid on it. "When I looked at all these points together," he said, "I began to see a pattern: a spiral, the center of which is in our own vicinity. You see the spiral, sir? They are out there, and they're coming *here*."

"Do you have any idea what you've got here, Singer?" said the general.

"Well, I have an inkling," said Singer, his voice oozing with false modesty.

"Bupkiss! Nothing! Good day!" thundered the general, already heading for the door.

Rentro, about to bite into his sandwich, decided that it was not a good moment and hid his lunch under the sofa cushion.

"But sir, we have to act now!" Singer protested.

"Singer, I hired you to find me an alien. And you show me doctored photos and a spiral? You're on thin ice, boy." Luft turned on his heel and left the room.

Singer was crushed. "Why is it men of vision are always laughed at?" he said bitterly. "They laughed at Newton, Galileo, Copernicus . . ."

". . . Seinfeld," added Rentro sympathetically, patting his boss's shoulder. "They were all very funny. You're in good company, sir."

When Singer glared at him, Rentro removed his hand from Singer's shoulder. A web of marshmallow fluff stretched between his paw and Singer's black jacket. Rentro shrugged and patted Singer's shoulder some more.

● ● ●

Meanwhile, back at the Muppet boarding house, Kermit, Fozzie, Clifford, Rizzo, and Animal were sitting around the dining room table, waiting for dinner.

Kermit stared out the window, worried about Gonzo. "What is he doing up there?" he asked.

"He's looking for something," said Fozzie helpfully.

"Hopefully his marbles!" said Clifford.

Miss Piggy swept into the room. "So exhausting to be in the limelight!" she said. "I'd love to sit and chat, but I need my beauty sleep! Ta-ta!"

Pepe entered the room with a huge crown roast. He placed it on the table with a flourish. "Eat up, gentlemen," he said.

"This is crazy," said Kermit. "Gonzo's been up there all day."

"You're right. He must be starving," said Rizzo quickly. "I'll bring him something." And before anyone could get any food, Rizzo swiped the entire crown roast and scooted away with it.

Up on the roof, Gonzo was still staring through the toy telescope. His attention was riveted on the sky. He was waiting.

Rizzo, now greatly fattened on crown roast, struggled to climb up onto the roof. In his hand, he carried one little rib. It was all that was left. He sat down and offered it to Gonzo.

"Hey, I brought you this," he said. "It's all I could rescue from those ruthless scavengers."

Gonzo was too absorbed to notice Rizzo's usual rascally behavior.

"Oh! Thanks, Rizzo." He took the rib but didn't eat it.

"Yeah, sure. So, what are you doing up here anyway?"

"Hey!" said Gonzo, pointing distractedly up at the sky. "Is that a . . . ? Oh, nope, just another bird."

"Look, Gonzo," said Rizzo, "you got friends down-stairs—they're concerned, ya know?" He paused to belch. "*I'm* concerned," he added.

"You know," said Gonzo, still looking at the sky, "I've always wondered where I came from, who I am. I finally feel like I'm close to getting some answers. I just know it!"

"Oh. Well, don't you think you oughta take a break? I mean, you're starting to freak out the neighbors."

"No, I have to stay here. I don't want to miss anything," Gonzo replied.

"Whatever you say, buddy," said Rizzo. He stared at the rib in Gonzo's hand. "So, uh, you going to eat that, or what?" he asked.

"Huh? Oh, no, it's all yours."

Rizzo didn't hesitate for a second. He darted for the rib, slipped, and slid off the roof, screaming. He landed with a thud.

"Are you okay?" Gonzo called down.

"Yeah," Rizzo replied. "My head broke the fall."

Later that night, Gonzo was still sitting on the roof. Suddenly a small bolt of lightning lit up the sky. Gonzo put the telescope down so he could look at it with his naked eye. The lightning darted from star to star, zigging and zagging. It got larger and larger, until—

Zzzztt! A huge, blinding flash of bright blue lightning zapped down from above and struck Gonzo, hard.

"*Ahhhhhhhhhhhh!*" he screamed. He was swallowed up by a cloud of blue smoke—and when it cleared, he was no longer on Earth but flying through space! Ahead of him, Gonzo saw two fish swimming through the sky. He flew up to them.

"Greetings, Mr. Gonzo!" they said. "We are cosmic-knowledge fish. We know many things."

Gonzo stared at them, his mouth open.

"Your people have been trying to reach you," said one of the fish. "You must respond if you wish to find what you seek."

The fish began to sing and dance. Gonzo watched in amazement. Then he suddenly started to fall. Gonzo's arms and legs flailed as he slammed into Earth's atmosphere, and everything went black. When he came to, Gonzo's clothes were blackened, his nose was bent into a corkscrew, his fur was burned and smoking, and his eyes were crossed and glowing. But he had a huge grin on his face.

"*Of course!*" he cried. "*That's it!*"

Downstairs, Kermit, Rizzo, Pepe, and Clifford were sitting around the dining room table, playing poker. There was a huge jackpot of food and junk in the middle of the table. For everyone in the house, no time at all had passed during the flash of lightning that had taken Gonzo across space and time.

"I'll see your two Maryland crab cakes and raise you a 1958 Camembert, never been sniffed," Rizzo said to Clifford. He put it on the table, his hands trembling. Rizzo could barely contain his excitement over the four aces he was holding.

"Too rich for my blood," said Kermit.

"Me too, man," said Clifford.

The door swung open, and there stood Gonzo, a charred, twisted mess, his fur still smoking. Kermit and Clifford stared at him in disbelief. Rizzo and Pepe were intent on the game and didn't look up.

"You guys!" Gonzo announced excitedly. "I know where I come from! I'm from outer space!"

"That's great," said Rizzo, not looking up from his cards. "Pepe, you in?"

"Oh yeah," said Pepe. "Whatta you got?"

Gonzo ran up to the table. "I'm an alien!"

Rizzo turned to look at him. "Jumpin' Jack O'Diamonds!" he exclaimed. "You look terrible!"

"I'm okay, really. I feel great!" replied Gonzo. He placed a reassuring hand on Rizzo's shoulder, zapping him so hard he flew out of his chair in a burst of smoke.

A moment later, Rizzo emerged from the smoke cloud with his fur singed, his whiskers bent. He looked down at his four aces, which had burst into flames. "Aaaaah! No! My cards!" he shrieked. He tried blowing them out, but they burned up in a flash, leaving him sobbing at the ashes in his hands.

Gonzo started rummaging around in the hardware drawer. He picked up a lightbulb. It glowed.

"Are you *sure* you're okay, Gonzo?" Kermit asked.

"Yeah, yeah! Absolutely! But I have to respond! Gotta make contact!" He finally found what he was looking for in the drawer: a ring of keys. Looking possessed, he walked purposefully to the door.

Clifford stared after him. "Where's he going with those keys?" he asked.

"To his flying saucer, okay?" said Pepe. He laid down his cards. "Pair of deuces—I win!"

Outside, Gonzo started up the lawn tractor. He began driving it, staring ahead, his face lit from below by the tractor's glowing dials. He swung the steering wheel crazily to the left and the right, driving, driving, driving....

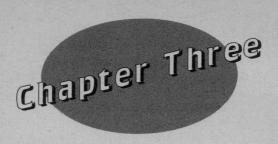

Chapter Three

Once Rizzo had recovered from his big poker loss, he and Pepe went outside to see what Gonzo was doing. The lawn tractor had driven up against the house, but the engine was still running. Gonzo was fast asleep at the wheel, snoring.

"This is not good," said Rizzo, shaking his head sadly. He reached over and turned off the engine. "Poor guy. He's hallucinating, getting weird messages, hearing things. We've got to do something."

They helped Gonzo off the tractor and walked him back to the house. Halfway there, they stopped and slowly turned to each other. "Wait a second," said Pepe. "Hold your horseshoes. I'm getting an idea."

● ● ●

Hours later, Gonzo was lying on his bed asleep. All at once, an eerie, wobbly voice began speaking to him. "Build it," said the voice, "and we will come!"

Gonzo stirred but did not quite wake up.

"Build...what?" he mumbled.

"Build—a Jacuzzi," Pepe responded, thinking fast, "and we will come, okaaaay." He was hiding on the floor behind Gonzo's bed, talking into a fan that distorted his voice in a spooky way.

"Okay," said Gonzo, hauling himself out of bed, still nine-tenths asleep. "I'm up, I'm up." He shuffled off to obey the alien command he'd heard in his sleep.

Watching him leave, Pepe and Rizzo high-fived each other joyously.

● ● ●

It wasn't long before Rizzo and Pepe were relaxing in the hot tub Gonzo had built, happily sipping cold beverages as they sat in the steaming water. And they weren't the only ones! Everyone was hanging out in and around the bubbling Jacuzzi. The Electric Mayhem band jammed nearby. It was party time!

"He built it. . ." cackled Rizzo.

". . . and we came!" Pepe finished, laughing uncontrollably. They clinked glasses and laughed some more.

Gonzo, wearing a tuxedo, was circulating the party like a nervous host. Every few moments, he looked up at the sky. "I want to impress my alien family," he said fretfully. "So try not to spill anything." He scanned the sky hopefully. But nothing unusual appeared.

Suddenly Rizzo felt terribly guilty. "We gotta tell him the truth, Pepe," he whispered. But Pepe didn't think that was such a good idea—they were having too much fun.

Inside the house, Kermit was sitting at his desk, watching Gonzo run around anxiously outside. Kermit was worried. Gonzo was acting weirder than usual.

● ● ●

Back at Covnet, Rentro stumbled into Singer's office, holding a stack of packages and videos. As usual, he had been temporarily blinded by the retinal scanner, so he walked cautiously with one arm outstretched, frequently bumping into the walls.

"Okay…," Rentro began, "just a few items for today, then. Let's see, your 'Platinum Buns' workout tape. Good news. Your Rogaine is in. Gotta love that! That new satellite photo is in your in-tray—"

"What satellite photo?" asked Singer sharply. He picked up the photo. Then he smiled.

The photo had been taken from very high in the air, but it was easy to see the words that Gonzo had mowed into the grass outside the Muppet boarding house: I AM HERE.

Singer grinned excitedly as he examined the photo

with a magnifying glass. "'I am here.' We have a response, Rentro! This is big! Only one thing has me confused."

"What's that, sir?"

"What are a rat and a shrimp doing in a Jacuzzi?"

Rentro looked closer. "They appear to be sipping drinks, sir."

"Okay, then," said Singer. "I want our men patrolling the area, secretly. Let's not scare anyone away. We're just watching and waiting."

Rentro stood frozen in place.

"What are you doing?" Singer barked.

"I'm watching and waiting," replied Rentro.

"Not you, Rentro!" shouted Singer.

"Ooh! Sorry," said the bear.

• • •

At the Muppet boarding house, things were busy. Nobody even noticed the black government car cruising by outside.

Dr. Bunsen Honeydew and his trusty scientific assistant, Beaker, had hooked Gonzo up to a bunch of wires, which were attached to a colander on Gonzo's head.

Gonzo looked worried. "I don't understand why they didn't show up last night," he said.

"Well, perhaps we can be of assistance," said Bunsen, fiddling with Gonzo's nose. "I think we can contact your alien friends if we boost your newly increased electrical conductivity and use your nose as a directional antenna."

"Thanks for helping me, guys. You're my last hope," said Gonzo through his pinched nose.

"Meep mee meep mohhh!" said Beaker.

"Good idea, Beaker," said Bunsen. "Let's give it some juice." He threw a switch. Nothing happened. "Maybe we need to apply some resistance," he said. "Beakie, hold this wire!"

Beaker started meeping in protest, but it was to no avail. Bunsen handed him a wire and threw the switch again, sending Beaker into spasms as electricity coursed through his body. Smoke came out of his ears.

"Excellent work, Beakie!" said Bunsen. He leaned closer to Gonzo. "How's that?" he asked.

"Great! I hear them! Can they hear me?" Gonzo moved a little. "It gets clearer when I move my arm!" he said.

"Fascinating," said Bunsen. "Your whole body is acting as an antenna. If we could only encase you in a better reception medium . . ."

At that same moment, Fozzie, Pepe, Clifford, and Rizzo were sitting around the living room television, watching a cheesy commercial for a TV show.

"'UFO Mania' live!" yelled the announcer. "With Shelley Snipes! Coming up! New footage! New scientific data and live exclusive close-encounter interviews!" The ad showed a series of shots of aliens and spaceships, as well as a photo of the show's host, Shelley Snipes.

Then, for some reason, the power in the house suddenly began to dim, and the TV reception started to falter.

"The show that asks: Do aliens exist?" continued the announcer. "Are they among us?"

"Sí, they live with us, okay!" Pepe answered back.

"Yeah, sometimes they even borrow our underpants!" Rizzo added.

The announcer kept talking as the lights sputtered. "If you've had an alien encounter and would like to be interviewed . . ."

". . . come to 44 Bronson Lane," he finished. But this time, his voice could be heard in the Muppet Lab, where Gonzo, now wrapped completely in aluminum foil, was still connected to a smoking Beaker. Gonzo was receiving the sound from the TV!

"The mother ship is calling me home!" he cried. Breaking away from the wires, Gonzo ran up the stairs. Behind him, Beaker collapsed into a smoking heap.

Rizzo and Pepe were in the kitchen getting a snack. Rizzo still felt guilty about the Jacuzzi. "It was your idea," he said to Pepe. "You should tell him."

"Sí, I will tell him, okay?" replied Pepe.

Just then Gonzo shot past them, still wrapped in aluminum foil and wearing the colander hat.

"Hey, uh, Gonzo?" Rizzo started.

"I can't talk now, guys!" Gonzo sped past them and out the door.

A moment later they heard the tractor start up. "I think he's mowing the lawn again, okay?" said Pepe.

Gonzo chugged down the street. The mysterious black government sedan followed close behind. When Gonzo pulled the tractor up in front of the TV studio, the sedan pulled in behind him.

• • •

Inside the studio, Miss Piggy sat in front of a mirror. "And that's the way it is," she said in her best announcer voice. "This is Miss Piggy, saying good night, and have a great—"

She was startled from her daydream by a piercing voice. "Where's that pig with my coffee?" it shrieked. It was Miss Piggy's boss, Sandy, the producer of the "UFO Mania" TV show.

"Oh! Coming! I'm coming!" Miss Piggy responded.

Before she could reach Sandy with the coffee, the stage manager ran up to him, yelling, "Sandy! Shelley's still stuck at the airport. She'll never make it here in time!"

Sandy took a deep breath. The host of his show was

missing. "Okay. I'm not going to panic," he said. "Who am I kidding? Yes I am. No. No I'm not. Let's see. Who can we possibly get at this late hour? Who?"

"Café au lait?" said Miss Piggy sweetly, knocking the stage manager out of the way in her haste to call attention to herself. "Ah hahahah," she laughed fetchingly.

In ten minutes, Miss Piggy was sitting behind the "UFO Mania" anchor desk, which was designed to look like a meteor split in two. The "UFO Mania" theme music started.

The stage manager began counting down to Miss Piggy's opening. "We're on in five, four, three. . ." The stage lights came up, and...

There was silence. Miss Piggy was frozen.

"Mmmmmmmmmmm," she said.

The stage manager stood next to the camera, holding up cue cards. Sandy was standing next to him. "Read!" he hissed loudly.

Awkwardly and slowly, Miss Piggy began reading the cards.

"Hello . . . again. I'm . . . Shelley Snipes . . ."

Sandy slapped his forehead. This was going to be a disaster.

• • •

At the boarding house, an exhausted Kermit plopped down in front of the TV with his friends.

"Whew! It feels great to finally relax," he said. He turned his attention to the TV and did a double take. Was that Miss Piggy?

Indeed it was. "Today on 'UFO Mania,' flying saucers," she was saying, "and their extraterrestrial pilots."

"Hey look, it's Piggy's new show!" shouted Fozzie.

Kermit stared at the screen in disbelief. "Piggy?"

A picture of a UFO appeared on the screen next to Miss Piggy. "I'm sure you've often wondered: What might these alien creatures look like?"

Suddenly she was interrupted by Gonzo, who popped in front of the camera, still clad in his aluminum-foil outfit.

"People of Earth, do not be alarmed!" he announced. "My message will be brief. I am Gonzo."

Miss Piggy couldn't believe her eyes. "Gonzo?" she said.

"Piggy?" said Gonzo, equally amazed.

Back at home, everybody was staring at Gonzo on TV, stunned. "Dang," said Clifford. "You'd better get down there, Kerm." Naturally, he assumed that Kermit would take care of the problem.

But this time, Kermit lost it. "What? Why do I always have to take care of everything and everybody? I've had it! No more! End of discussion."

On television, Gonzo was explaining everything to his Earthling audience. "...You see, I was contacted through my breakfast cereal. It's now clear to me that I am from outer space."

Everyone stared at Kermit. Rizzo finally spoke. "So," he said to Kermit, "should we go now or wait till the commercial?"

"Now," Kermit answered.

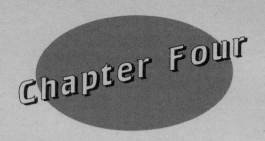

Chapter Four

At the secret-government-agency-pretending-to-be-a-concrete-company, Rentro was sitting at Singer's desk, pretending to be the boss. Spinning around in the chair, he used the remote to turn on the TV and started channel surfing. "Boobadoop-doo," he hummed to himself as he flipped. "Boring. Nope. Ooh, this looks good." It was "UFO Mania."

"What would you like to know?" Gonzo asked Miss Piggy.

"I want to know everything!" said Miss Piggy. "The whole tearful tale of your inner struggle."

Rentro's viewing was interrupted by Singer, who had entered his office and was glaring at the bear. "Rentro, we're not here for your amusement! Turn that off!" he ordered.

Rentro leaped out of his seat. "Oh, uh…" he began. Just then, Singer spotted Gonzo on TV.

"…and that's why I came down here, Piggy," Gonzo

was saying. "I'm here because I want my people to know I've received their messages. And my response to them is: I am here!"

Singer stared at the TV. "'I am here,'" he repeated. "Bingo!"

"I'm at 44 Bronson Lane," Gonzo continued. "And I can't wait to meet you!"

Singer smiled a cold smile. "And I can't wait to meet *you*," he said.

• • •

Meanwhile, back on the "UFO Mania" set, Kermit and Rizzo had arrived.

"Gonzo," said Rizzo.

"Kermie?" said Miss Piggy.

"Piggy," said Kermit.

"What the heck is going on here?" said Sandy.

"Gonzo, aren't you taking this alien thing too far?" asked Kermit. "You're starting to worry us."

Gonzo shook his head. "Kermit," he began, "I realize it may be hard for you to accept me as an alien. I didn't ask to be an alien. But I've always had alien tendencies, and now it just makes sense to me...."

Sandy spoke up. "That's beautiful, Big G," he said. "I see a follow-up episode here—"

Miss Piggy interrupted him. "Me too!" she said. "Friends of Gonzo: A Miss Piggy Special Report."

Sandy shot her a look.

"We'll take this from here," interrupted a voice.

Everyone turned. There in the doorway were two men in black: black suits, dark glasses, the works.

"I'm Agent Barker," said one of them. "We're with the Society for the Prevention of Cruelty to Aliens. We feel your pain."

"That's wonderful! They feel my pain!" said Gonzo. He turned to Agent Barker. "Can you help me make contact with my alien tribe?" he asked.

"Yes, we can, Gonzo," said Agent Barker.

Kermit stepped between the men in black and Gonzo. "Gonzo," he said, "just because you're different, that doesn't make you an alien."

"Well, somebody believes me," said Gonzo. He walked over to the men. "Come on, fellas. Take me to my leader!"

As he walked away with them, Rizzo shook his head. "I don't like the look of these guys. This rat smells a rat!"

"The limo is right this way," said Agent Barker to Gonzo.

"Did he say 'limo'?" asked Rizzo. That changed everything! He darted after Gonzo and the men in black. "Hey, wait up, guys!" he shouted. "I'm his translator."

The group in the studio was left staring.

"You actually know this Gonzo, right?" Sandy asked Miss Piggy.

Miss Piggy's mind was already going a mile a minute. "I might if the price is right," she said.

"Price?" asked Sandy.

Miss Piggy grabbed Sandy's tie and pulled him down to her level.

"I give you the exclusive story on Gonzo, and you make moi the new anchorwoman," she said.

"But what about Shelley?" asked Sandy.

"Shelley, smelly," said Miss Piggy.

Sandy thought for a brief moment. "Yes, yes. Go!" he said. Miss Piggy squealed with excitement as she ran off.

As soon as she got outside, Miss Piggy tore after the two men who were escorting Gonzo and Rizzo away. She had not forgotten her reporter's pad and pen.

"A-hem! Oh, cruelty people? Where are you taking Gonzo?" she called out.

Agent Barker turned to his co-man-in-black. "I'll deal with her," he said quietly. The other agent walked off with Gonzo and Rizzo while Barker turned to face Miss Piggy. He looked her up and down appraisingly.

Miss Piggy was mad. "Deal with moi? Look chump-o, I'm just trying to get a story here."

"How about this story?" said Agent Barker. "It's about a big bad wolf and a little pig." He moved closer to Miss Piggy.

"There were *three* little pigs," said Miss Piggy.

"Not in this version," said Barker.

Miss Piggy looked at him suspiciously, stepping backward as he moved closer. "Who are you, and where are you taking Gonzo?" she demanded.

Agent Barker just smiled and grabbed her arm. But Miss Piggy was ready. Dropping the pen and pad and pulling away from Barker's grip, she immediately went into full karate stance.

"I'm impressed," said Agent Barker. He whirled around and kicked a nearby crate, sending it flying. Then he smiled captivatingly. "Black belt. Third degree," he murmured.

In response, Miss Piggy karate-chopped some nearby two-by-fours, snapping them cleanly in half.

"Platinum belt with an unlimited line of credit," she explained sweetly, pointing to herself.

Agent Barker whipped off his jacket. They faced off. They exchanged a few blows, each coolly blocking the other's attack.

Barker was smitten. "Where have you been all my life?" he asked.

• • •

Kermit walked up the path to the Muppet boarding house. But what was this? For some reason, a large crowd was assembled on the front lawn.

Sam the Eagle was out on the porch, trying to shoo them all away. But they weren't going. A few of them held up large signs. On the signs were pictures of Gonzo.

"No, there are no aliens here," Sam was explaining in exasperation. The two chickens at his side squawked in agreement. "Only good, old-fashioned, hard-working Americans. Now, get off my Kentucky bluegrass!"

As Kermit came down the front walk, a kid on a bike pointed at him. "Hey! It's a little green man!" he yelled.

"What are you people doing here?" Kermit asked them.

A loony-looking woman stepped forward, holding a dish with a pile of mashed potatoes on it. The mashed potatoes were sculpted to look like Gonzo's head. "We were drawn here by the alien," she said blissfully.

"Now get out of here," said Sam. "All of you. Get out of here before I run out of patience!"

Nobody moved.

• • •

On the "UFO Mania" set, Agent Barker was now tied up, with a black eye. Miss Piggy, looking none the worse for wear, sat beside him, feeding him grapes. A bottle of wine and some cheese sat nearby.

". . . I swear, that's all I know," said Agent Barker.

"So...this government agency, Covnet, has abducted Gonzo and taken him to its top-secret facility?" said Miss Piggy.

"Yes, Miss Piggy," he said.

"Thank you, darling. You've been most helpful." Miss Piggy had a faraway look in her eyes. "At last! A real story! Intrigue, danger, new outfits. And it's all mine! Mine! Mine!"

She ran out. Agent Barker looked confused. "Uh-oh!" he said. "Wait! Don't leave! I thought we were soul mates!"

Miss Piggy hightailed it back to the boarding house. Kermit, Fozzie, Pepe, and Animal were sitting in the living room when she burst in, out of breath.

"Listen, everyone!" she panted. "I have great news. Gonzo and Rizzo have been kidnapped by the government, and it could be a life-threatening situation!"

"How is that great news?" Kermit inquired.

"Because I've got the story, I've got the story," chanted Miss Piggy in a singsongy voice. Then she headed for the stairs. "I need to change," she said. "Something that says journalistic integrity, but shows just a hint of skin."

"What are we going to do?" asked Fozzie.

"This thing has gone way too far," said Kermit to the others. "How are *we* going to save Gonzo from an army of government agents?"

"I have a joke book," offered Fozzie. "Comedy can be a very effective weapon, you know?"

"I've got some loose Jell-O, okay?" said Pepe, pulling a quivering orange cube from his pocket.

"Drum-sticks! Drum-sticks!" bellowed Animal, waving them around.

"Okay," said Kermit. "In circumstances like this, there's only one place to turn…"

It was time for a visit to Muppet Labs, located in the basement of the boarding house.

Bunsen and Beaker were happy to help. Bunsen laid out several ordinary-looking objects on the countertop: Scotch Tape, a rubber ducky, a perfume spray bottle, and a jar. Kermit and the gang gathered around for a demonstration.

"What have you got, Bunsen?" asked Kermit.

"Well, Kermit, we've come up with a number of devices which should aid you in your secret operations." First Bunsen held up the rubber ducky. "This seemingly ordinary rubber ducky actually contains Invisibility Spray. However, the effect lasts only a few minutes."

"The ol' rubber-duck-with-Invisibility-Spray trick . . . check!" said Kermit.

Next, Bunsen handed the jar to Kermit. "And here's something we're very excited about," he said.

Kermit read the label. "Door in a Jar?"

"Yes, that's right. All you do is open up the jar, fling

   39

the contents onto a wall, and, voilà! Instant door."

"Somehow I have a feeling that's going to come in mighty handy," said Kermit.

Fozzie picked up the Scotch Tape. "What is this?" he asked. "A secret communication device?" He tried talking into it: "Hello, Fozzie to base, Fozzie to base."

"No, that's Scotch Tape," said Bunsen. "Very useful if something tears."

"And what do you have for moi?" asked Miss Piggy, suddenly appearing in the doorway. For her big reporter assignment, she was wearing a completely over-the-top outfit.

"Ah, Miss Piggy," said Bunsen. "For you we have Muppet Labs Mind Mist. Spray it on the subject and expect them to obey your every command." He picked up the perfume spray bottle. Miss Piggy stepped forward to take it, tripped clumsily, and then dropped the bottle into her purse.

"I doubt I'll need it," she said confidently.

It was time to get going. "Let's go get Gonzo!" said Kermit.

"And get the scoop that will launch my career!" Miss Piggy added.

The others ignored her—and hurried out of the basement.

*T*he black government sedan pulled up at the gate of Covnet, aka the AAA Cement Company.

The guard opened the gate and the sedan passed through. When they got inside the building, Gonzo and Rizzo were escorted down the hall by the man in black and two armed guards.

At last they arrived at Singer's office. The door opened—and Singer stood there, his arms open wide in greeting.

"Welcome! As an ambassador of Earth, I welcome you!" he said. "I must say, I'm honored to meet you, Mr. Gonzo. I'm Edgar—Ed, if you like." He quickly put on a rubber glove and shook Gonzo's hand.

"Oh thanks, Ed," said Gonzo. "So you guys going to help me contact my alien tribe?"

"I've spent my entire life looking for something like you," said Singer. "If you could call it a life." Singer smiled broadly. "Please, sit," he said.

Gonzo sat down, and Singer began to circle him, staring curiously, studying him. Then he held his finger inches away from Gonzo's nose. "May I?" he asked.

"Before he answers," said Rizzo, "I'd suggest you be very clear on the final destination of that finger!"

Singer gently touched Gonzo's snout, squeezed it, and then twisted it hard as if to see if it was a fake. "Hmmm. No nostrils. How do you smell?"

"Awful!" said Rizzo. "Trust me, I'm his roommate."

This got a laugh from Rentro and Gonzo. Singer chuckled briefly, but then he suddenly snapped. "*Please don't laugh at me!*" he screamed.

Rentro stepped in. "I thought you were just great on TV," he said to Gonzo. "Do you think I could get your autograph? It's not for me. Okay, it's for me."

"Rentro! Not a good time!" yelled Singer. Rentro skulked away, and Singer turned back to Gonzo.

"Please forgive my Earthly manners," said Singer. "It's just... Do you know what it's like to be laughed at?"

"Sure," replied Gonzo.

"To be called names like 'wacko'?"

"Uh-huh."

"And 'freak'?" Singer added.

"Oh yeah," said Gonzo.

"'Paranoid delusional psychopath'?"

"Got me there," said Gonzo.

Singer wasn't done. "To feel completely alone in this world?" he said.

"I think we're gettin' the picture there, Ed," said Rizzo, doing the finger circle for "crazy."

Singer closed his eyes and sighed in frustration. Rizzo was getting on his nerves. Singer pressed a button on his desk, and a huge bodyguard stepped into the office.

"Have the rat sent down to Dr. Tucker for some tests," Singer said to the bodyguard.

Rizzo started to panic. "Tests? But I haven't studied. I don't even have a number two pencil!"

The bodyguard walked over to Rizzo, picked him up by the tail, and took him over to a garbage-chute-like drawer. He opened it and dropped Rizzo inside. Gonzo jumped up from his chair. "Hey—what are you doing with my friend?" he said.

Whoosh! Rizzo was gone, but Gonzo could hear him yelling as he plummeted downward: "*Gonzooooooooo . . .!*"

●　●　●

Rizzo fell for a long time, yelling all the way. Then he bumped and slid and fell some more, through a long series of tubes, until at last he dropped unceremoniously into a rat cage.

When he looked up, he found himself in the company of six other rats. They were a tough-looking, scarred-up bunch. Many of them sported Band-Aids, eye patches, and ice packs. One had an arm in a sling. A couple of muscular types were bench-pressing weights. Another sat on a bunk playing the harmonica. The popular "Mice Girls" poster hung on their wall. It was more like a prison cell than a rat cage.

The lead rat, a huge, overweight rodent, extended a paw in greeting. "Yo," he said. "I'm Bubba." He pointed out some of the other rats. "That's Fast Eddie, Red, Shakes"—he indicated a rat who was shaking nervously—"they're testing a caffeine substitute on him. And that's the Birdman. He's been here forever; he don't bother anybody. Just wants to be left alone with his birds." Bubba was pointing to an older, mild-mannered rat with glasses. The Birdman held a crumb in his paw. A pigeon twice his size landed on him, knocked him down, and started pecking at him.

"And that's about all of us here in Medical Research," Bubba concluded.

"Medical Research?" cried Rizzo with dread. "That means we're . . . lab rats?"

$$\bullet \quad \bullet \quad \bullet$$

Upstairs, Gonzo was having his own troubles. He was now face-to-face with Singer, who plucked out one of Gonzo's hairs with tweezers, examining it as he talked. Gonzo looked scared.

"When were you first contacted?" said Singer.

"I. . . Uh, let me think. I guess it started when I had Kap'n Alphabet for breakfast—"

"I see," said Singer. "And who is this Kap'n Alphabet?"

"He's a cereal," replied Gonzo.

"A cereal," said Singer thoughtfully. "Okay."

Singer flipped the switch on his remote control. All of the photos of the R U THERE? sightings came up on the monitors. "Maybe you wouldn't mind telling me about…" He spun Gonzo's chair around to face the monitors. "These!"

"Whoa! They've really been looking for me," said Gonzo in amazement.

"How many are there? Hordes? Legions?"

"I don't know," replied Gonzo.

"What is their agenda?"

"I don't know," said Gonzo.

"When are they coming?" But before Gonzo could answer, Singer snapped again. "*And don't tell me you don't know!*" he shrieked.

"I . . . know not?" Gonzo tried.

Singer glared at him.

"But maybe I can find out?" Gonzo added quickly.

"Oh, do you think you could?" said Singer.

"Sure," said Gonzo. He got up from his chair and headed for the door. "Okay then, I'll keep in touch. Thanks for everything."

Singer calmly watched Gonzo hurry toward the door. When he got there, the door slid open, revealing the same huge bodyguard. He was standing squarely in Gonzo's way.

"Oh, don't bother, I can see myself out," said Gonzo hopefully. The bodyguard growled at him. "Or you could just point the way...."

Singer spoke up. "It's a shame, really. I admire you for trying to protect your people, and yet, I need the information which you so closely guard. We're just going to have to perform an invasive quadralobal brain probe on you and pluck it from your head."

Gonzo gulped, gently shielding his head with his hands. "'It' being...the information?" he asked.

"No. Your brain! Take him away please!"

The bodyguard began to pull Gonzo away backward. "Wait, I really don't know anything!" Gonzo squawked. "Stop! I need my brain! *Rizzooooooo!*"

• • •

Meanwhile, Rizzo's situation was also getting worse by the minute. He had just met Dr. Tucker, the wardenlike scientist in charge of the lab.

"Hello, fresh meat," said the doctor, looming scarily over Rizzo. "My name is Dr. Tucker. From this moment on, you're mine. If I say you're hungry, you eat. If I say you're sleepy—"

"We eat?" ventured Rizzo helpfully.

"Well, well, well, we've got us a funny boy here. I guess I'm gonna have to put funny boy in the maze. And since we don't want funny boy here to get lonely, you can *all* do some time in the maze."

The other lab rats trembled in fear as Tucker leaned toward them evilly. "No one has ever escaped from the maze, funny boy. And even it you did, it's four feet down to the floor, twelve feet to the door, and another four feet up to the doorknob. Funny thing about doorknobs: rats can't turn 'em. No opposable thumb." Dr. Tucker wiggled his thumb in Rizzo's face and laughed a wicked laugh.

"Well, at least *we* don't have kitty litter breath," Rizzo wisecracked.

The next thing Rizzo knew, he and the others were running around inside the rat maze, trying to find their way out. As Rizzo rounded a corner, Bubba stuck his head over the wall to warn him. "Don't step on the red circles!"

"What's wrong with the red—?" Rizzo stepped on a red circle. Instantly, he was zapped with a jolt of electricity. The voltage sent him flying out of the maze. He crashed back down, smoking. Bubba just watched, shaking his head.

"God bless America," Rizzo chattered nonsensically. "I didn't do nothin'! I didn't do nothin'! I like cheese!"

Having flunked that test, Rizzo went on to the

next. He sat at a desk inside a small observation room. On one side of the desk was a large wedge of delicious-looking cheese. On the other side was a box marked RAT POISON.

Rizzo looked from one side to the other. "Ha!" he said. "What do you think I am—stupid? Like I can't read! This is a no-brainer!" He reached confidently for the cheese. As soon as he touched it, a large boxing glove flew out of nowhere and punched him, hard.

A long series of experiments followed, all involving similarly bad surprises at the end. Rizzo was not having any fun at all.

Chapter Six

A couple of miles away, the Electric Mayhem bus was moving down the road. Fozzie was driving, and Animal, Pepe, Kermit, and Miss Piggy were his passengers. Kermit gazed thoughtfully out the window.

"Piggy," he said, "I just feel terrible about Gonzo and Rizzo. I can't imagine anything bad happening to those guys."

"Really?" said Miss Piggy.

"I should have recognized the signs that he was losing it. But with Gonzo, who can tell?"

"Don't worry," said Miss Piggy, sitting at his left. "Everything is going to be fine, I promise."

"Thanks, Piggy," he said, still staring out the window. "I really appreciate—"

"Okay, Sandy," said Miss Piggy, who had been talking into her cell phone the whole time. "I'm going undercover now. I'll make contact when it's safe. Over and out. Copy. Ten-four."

Kermit just looked disgusted as Miss Piggy hung up the phone, beaming excitedly at her friends. When they all laughed, she glared at them.

Up front, Pepe was talking to Fozzie. "Tell me again, why are we doing this?" he asked.

"To save Gonzo," Fozzie replied.

"Gonzo! Gonzo!" chanted Animal. Everyone nodded in agreement.

"That's right. Gonzo's one of us," said Kermit. "And no matter what happens, no matter what obstacles we face, we never forget one of our own!"

Everybody cheered. Then, a minute later, Pepe leaned over to Fozzie. "Tell me again, why are we doing this?" he asked.

• • •

Gonzo sat in a bare holding cell, looking depressed. After a while, the narrow slot in his door opened. Rentro stuck his snout in.

"Pssst! Room service."

Rentro opened the door and entered the cell. "Here's a peanut butter, banana, and pickle sandwich. I even cut off the crusts for ya," he said sympathetically.

"Thanks a lot," said Gonzo sadly.

"Hey, no problem," said Rentro, trying to cheer Gonzo up. "Anything for a celebrity. Ooh! Do you like jalapeños?"

"Sure."

"I'll be right back," said Rentro, closing the cell door behind him.

Gonzo put his sandwich down on the cot and sighed. "I guess this is the end of the line, the grand finale," he said to himself. "Poor Rizzo. Wherever you are pal, I'm sorry."

"Hey, mopey!" said a voice.

"Who said that?" said Gonzo.

"I did," said Gonzo's sandwich.

"But you're a sandwich."

"I am merely channeling my voice through the sandwich," said the sandwich, "in order to deliver this message to you. We arrive at midnight tonight."

"Really! And do all of you look like sandwiches?"

"Forget about the sandwich! The sandwich is just a conduit!"

"Okay, sorry," said Gonzo to his new alien friend.

Meanwhile, Rentro had gotten a jar of jalapeños and was about to reenter Gonzo's cell when he heard voices inside. He stopped and listened.

"We are landing at your house!" said the sandwich.

"No, wait," said Gonzo, "you can't go there! These guys know where I live, and they're, well, they're not the best examples of Earthlings."

"Where else could we land?" asked the sandwich.

"Uh, let's see—oh, I know! Land at the beach! Go to Cape Doom! Just look for the lighthouse!"

Rentro looked around with concern. "The lighthouse at Cape Doom?" he repeated to himself. Then he left.

"This is so great!" Gonzo was saying to the sandwich. "But how do I get out of here?"

"Hey, I'm just a sandwich. Some things you got to figure out for yourself." After a moment the sandwich added, "By the way, you go ahead and eat me now. You'll need the energy."

"Won't that hurt?" Gonzo said worriedly.

"No, no, I'm going away now," replied the sandwich.

Gonzo picked up the sandwich and cautiously started to take a bite. Suddenly, the sandwich spoke again.

"You did say Cape Doom, right?"

"Whoa! Yes," said Gonzo. That was close. But the sandwich was quiet again. "Are you gone now? Hello?" he said.

He shrugged and opened his mouth to take a bite. But just then, the door opened ominously, and two guards wheeled in a scary-looking hospital gurney. Gonzo gulped.

● ● ●

Dr. Tucker was still having fun with the rats downstairs. He leaned down to talk to them in their cage. "Hey. Rodents. Remember all that cheese I promised you after you ran those mazes and took those tests? Well, it was delicious." He licked his fingers.

Later that night, Rizzo paced around the rat cage. He was fed up. "No cheese?" he screamed. "No cheese? That does it. We are bustin' out of this joint!"

Bubba shook his head in despair. "Even if we did go over the wall," he said, "we can't turn that doorknob."

"Who needs a doorknob?" asked Rizzo wickedly. He rolled up the "Mice Girls" poster that hung on the wall, revealing a ventilation grate that he'd partially removed.

"Right on!" said Bubba.

• • •

The Electric Mayhem bus pulled off the road before it got to the guard gate outside the cement factory.

A few minutes later, a bush began moving toward the guardhouse. Just visible behind the bush were Kermit, Miss Piggy, Fozzie, Animal, and Pepe.

Miss Piggy hurriedly fixed her hair. "Out of the way, boys," she whispered. "This is a job for a woman."

"Wo-man!" roared Animal.

"*Shhhhhh!*" everybody said.

Miss Piggy approached the guardhouse, whispering dramatically into a handheld tape recorder. "Ten forty P.M., Friday, Miss Piggy reporting. I am approaching the guard gate of the top-secret facility."

She reached the gate. "Hello-o-o," she said sweetly

to the guard. "What's a nice man like you doing in a guardhouse like this?"

"What's it look like I'm doing?" said the guard grumpily. "It's obvious. This is a restricted area, lady. You gotta go."

"Oh, pshaw. You don't want moi to leave, do vous?" She leaned over to touch him.

"Don't touch me!" he barked.

She tried another tack. "Look deeply into my eyes and tell me you want me to go."

The guard looked deep into her eyes. "I want you to go!" he said. "Now!"

"Humph!" said Miss Piggy, not moving. "A difficult situation, which obviously calls for my feminine wiles." She turned off her tape recorder and glanced over her shoulder to make sure the others weren't looking. Then she pulled out the spray bottle and spritzed the guard. "Open the gate, bub," she said.

"You got it, sweetie," said the guard, suddenly under the spell of Dr. Bunsen Honeydew's Mind Mist. "You just go right ahead into this top-secret facility." He pulled a lever, and the gate opened, allowing Miss Piggy through along with the others.

"Hey! Those your friends?" said the guard. "Hiya, fellas."

"Wow, that guard fell on you like a ton of bricks," said Pepe to Miss Piggy when they were inside.

"Naturellement!" she replied with her usual modesty.

• • •

Kermit and his friends were now hiding near the front entrance to the building. Armed guards were posted nearby.

"Okay. We have to get through that door," said Kermit, pointing.

"Should we just ask permission from those nice men with the rifles?" suggested Fozzie.

"Fozzie! They're the bad guys!" whispered Kermit.

"Ooh," said Fozzie.

"It's time to get invisible," said Kermit dramatically. "Fozzie, get the duck."

Fozzie pulled out the rubber ducky and sprayed the others. They slowly dissolved into invisibility.

"Now it's your turn, Fozzie," said the now-invisible Kermit.

Ffffft! Fozzie disappeared.

Invisible Kermit threw the ducky into the bushes, and they headed for the door.

"Okay, everybody," said Invisible Kermit when they were safely inside the building, "this invisibility spray doesn't last long. Let's go!"

"Yeah. Whatever we do, let's not waste any time!" Invisible Fozzie agreed.

Five minutes later, the whole invisible gang— except for Invisible Fozzie—was waiting outside the men's room. Inside, a toilet flushed. "Okay, Kermit,

I'm ready," said Invisible Fozzie when he finally came out.

But he wasn't completely invisible anymore. Everyone stared as a pair of brown paws floated in midair. "Er, Fozzie, you didn't by any chance wash your hands?" said Invisible Kermit.

"Of course I did! Mom said always wash your hands!"

"Not when you're wearing invisibility spray," said Invisible Kermit.

"Mom said no exceptions!" Invisible Fozzie protested.

They were interrupted by a female armed guard who had just come down the corridor and noticed the "floating" pair of hands. "You. Hands. Put 'em up," she ordered. She got out her cuffs and tried to grab at Fozzie's hands, but Fozzie kept moving them around.

"Help! Help!" he yelled in a panic.

Suddenly the guard jumped. Someone had pinched her!

"Wo-man! Wo-man!" bellowed the voice of Invisible Animal.

She jumped again and took off down the hall, Animal's voice trailing after her.

"I think we've lost Animal," said Invisible Fozzie.

"All right, everybody," said Invisible Kermit. "Hang on just a second. I need to think. He's not on this floor."

As Kermit was talking, he noticed that one finger

of Fozzie's hand was pointing at the ceiling. Gradually, more of Fozzie was becoming visible again. In fact, *all* of them were becoming visible! The spray was wearing off! And there was Fozzie, picking his nose. Embarrassed, he glanced around to see if any of the others were watching him. Kermit was staring right at him.

Miss Piggy wasn't, however. She was turned around, adjusting her underpants, not realizing that she could be seen. Pepe, for his part, was dancing like a ballerina and humming to himself. As the others realized that they were visible, Pepe kept on dancing, oblivious. Suddenly he noticed everyone was looking at him. Oops.

"Hello," he said, trying not to look embarrassed.

"Come on, guys," said Kermit. "We have to find some better cover!"

A couple of minutes later, two very tall doctors in white coats were waiting for the elevator—a frog doctor and a shrimp doctor. One of them had furry bear feet and the other was sporting a very stylish pair of high heels. Only an extremely observant onlooker would have noticed that the lab coats were lumpy and squirmy underneath.

Also waiting for the elevator were two men in black, hustling a seedy-looking fellow between them. It was Kap'n Alphabet, and he looked as if he'd seen better days.

"I tell ya, I'm just a cereal mascot!" he was yelling. "I don't know anything!"

"Don't give us any of your sugar-coated lies, Kap'n!" said one of his captors.

The elevator doors opened. Trying to maintain their balance, the very tall frog and shrimp doctors awkwardly shuffled out of the way as Kap'n Alphabet was escorted onto the elevator.

*I*n a brightly-lit operating room somewhere in the Covnet building, Gonzo lay strapped to a gurney, covered with a white sheet. Above him hung a large laser machine.

"Paging Dr. Van Neuter," intoned a pleasant voice over the intercom. "Please come to alien surgery suite five. Thank you."

The doorknob turned. The door opened. In came a sinister-looking doctor.

"Hello," he said to Gonzo. "My name is Dr. Phil Van Neuter. I'll be your brain surgeon today. I hope you don't mind. Get it? 'Brain surgeon?' 'Mind?'"

Gonzo was not in a laughing mood.

"It's a joke, silly!" said the doctor. "To put you at ease!"

"It's not working," mumbled Gonzo.

Dr. Phil leaned down toward Gonzo. "So, how are we feeling?" he inquired.

"Terrified," Gonzo replied.

"Well, everyone *is*, the first time. Let's take a look at your chart, shall we?" He picked up the clipboard at the foot of Gonzo's gurney. "Oh! An alien!" he cried joyously. "My first! Okay, just a few standard questions before we get started…. Now, do you have or have you ever experienced any achiness in your tentacles?"

Dr. Phil was so excited about working on his first alien, he didn't even notice the rope that was being lowered into the room behind him. Gonzo noticed it, though. It was inching out of the air duct in the ceiling.

"Uh . . . I don't have tentacles," he said, distractedly playing along with Dr. Phil.

"No achy tentacles! Excellent! Head ever come off?"

"Uh . . . I don't think so."

"Good. Gum disease?"

"No," said Gonzo. But he wasn't looking at the doctor. He was watching Rizzo, who was sliding down the rope behind the doctor! He had come to save Gonzo!

The doctor, not seeing a thing, tweaked Gonzo's nose. "How about that beaky thing you've got there? Any itching, swelling, or flaking?"

"Not really," said Gonzo, barely able to hide his excitement. Rizzo had dropped off the end of the rope.

"Alrighty then! It's showtime!" crowed the doctor. He tossed the chart aside and drew down the giant laser machine from the ceiling, twirled it with a flourish, and aimed it straight at Gonzo.

Gonzo thought fast. "Wait!" he cried.

"What is it?"

"Are you sure this is covered by my health insurance?"

This was a matter of genuine concern to the doctor. "Good question," he said. "I'll check."

He turned around to check Gonzo's chart, and while his back was turned, Rizzo climbed up onto Gonzo's gurney.

"Rizzo! You're alive!" whispered Gonzo. "Where've you been?"

"You don't wanna know. C'mon, I'm gettin' you outta here!"

The doctor turned back to Gonzo, and Rizzo ducked under the sheet. "Good news!" said Dr. Phil. "You're covered!" He smiled. "Please let me know if you experience any unpleasantness. I'd hate to miss it." He pulled back the sheet, all ready to start Gonzo's brain-removal surgery. But what was this?

It was Rizzo, chewing away on Gonzo's wrist strap, trying to free him.

"Do you mind?" said Rizzo.

"Oh, excuse me," said the doctor, letting go of the

sheet. Then he quickly pulled the sheet back again. "Good Lord!" he cried. "Ooh, I hate rats!"

"Then today ain't your lucky day, Doctor," said a voice. Dr. Phil spun around. There was Bubba, standing on an instrument tray and brandishing a cotton swab like a billy club. All the other lab rats stood behind him.

• • •

The very tall frog doctor and the very tall shrimp doctor moved jerkily down the hall in their lab coats. They tried to look casual as they walked along, peeking into doors.

A scientist passing by stopped to give them a strange look.

"Doctor!" said the frog doctor.

"Doctor!" said the shrimp doctor. "Yes, we're all just doctors hanging out here in the hallway," he added nonchalantly.

The scientist hurried off, glancing back at them in confusion.

"That was close, okay?" said the tall shrimp doctor.

Suddenly, they heard a voice echoing down the hallway. It sounded like a madman having a laughing attack. "Oh! Stop it! I can't take it!" the voice screeched.

Kermit and Pepe exchanged looks. "It's coming from in there," said Kermit, pointing to a door down the hall. They managed to shuffle over to the door marked OPERATING SUITE 5. Kermit and Pepe peered through the windows in the operating room door.

Inside was a very strange scene. There was Gonzo, struggling to free himself from the gurney straps. And there was a doctor, doubled over helplessly in painful laughter as a bunch of rats ran around inside his lab coat, furiously tickling him.

"I'll handle this. Stand back!" yelled Miss Piggy, jumping forward. This sent Kermit flying into the shrimp doctor, and everybody fell down.

Miss Piggy whipped out her tape recorder. "I, Miss Piggy, investigative reporter, am about to knock down this massive door," she announced into it, "and lead the others in rescuing the lone victim at the heart of this conspiracy."

During Miss Piggy's dramatic setup, however, her friends simply stood up, pushed through the swinging doors, and strolled into the operating room.

"Huh? Wait for me!" she said when she realized she was alone in the hallway. She raced through the door after them.

Dr. Phil was still being tickled by the rats. "Please!" he half wailed, half laughed. "Somebody help me! It's too muuuuuch!"

Rizzo was still working on the straps that held Gonzo down. "I can't chew through them!" he said. "Someone grab the gurney!"

"Quick! Get me out of here!" Gonzo begged them.

Leaving Dr. Phil behind, still screaming with laughter, Kermit and the others pushed Gonzo's gurney out into the hallway. Rizzo rode on it with Gonzo.

At that moment, Singer was escorting General Luft down the hallway to the operating room. They turned a corner, just missing a view of the gurney being pushed away.

"Dr. Van Neuter should have the alien anesthetized by now," Singer was explaining gleefully to his boss. "This is big, General. I think we should notify the President."

"I'll be the judge of that," said the general.

The two men arrived at the operating theater, and Singer pointed to the window, looking very pleased with himself. "I find that most of the time people think with their little minds…. Well, today it's time to think with the big mind."

The operating room was filled with an eerie blue smoke. Singer smiled in anticipation.

Suddenly, Dr. Phil flew up into the window, flattening his face against it. He was laughing insanely, beating at the rats rustling under his coat. "Ahahahahh! The nibbling! The tiny nibbling!" he screeched.

"Er—this looks worse than it is, General," the panic-stricken Singer said quickly. "The alien is obviously loose in the building, but he won't get past security."

"Don't bother, Singer. I've seen enough," said the general disgustedly. "You're terminated."

"But sir—"

The general cut him off. "You need help. Find some." Then he stormed away.

Along came Rentro. He looked with curiosity at his boss, who was on the verge of hyperventilating.

"Breathe, sir," said Rentro helpfully. "Deep breaths. Let it go. Calm blue oceans."

Singer lost it. "I am through playing these reindeer games! Find the alien! *Now!*" he thundered.

• • •

In another part of the building, Kermit, Pepe, Fozzie, and Miss Piggy were running down the hall, along with Gonzo and Rizzo. They had gotten rid of the gurney. "Thanks for coming to save me, guys," said Gonzo. "I'm sorry I put you through all this."

"You can thank us once we're safely out of here, Gonzo," said Kermit.

Suddenly they heard shouting nearby. They ducked quickly into a doorway.

It was Animal, who was tearing around the corner with the female guard close behind him. "You can't leave me! I need you—you—animal!" She caught up with

Animal, grabbed him, and pulled him into a bear hug.

He finally pulled free and barreled down the hall toward his beckoning friends. "Woman! Tiring!" Animal said, exhausted.

Now that the Muppets were all together, they took off down the hallway. But a group of guards was now rushing toward them.

"*Aaaahhhh!*" the Muppets screamed. They turned and ran, and as they went around a bend, they saw yet another group of guards coming at them from the other direction!

"*Aaaahhhh!*" they all screamed again. They froze in fear. They had nowhere to run.

"I was tired of running anyway," panted Fozzie.

"No!" said Gonzo as the guards closed in. "There's gotta be a way out!"

"Quick, Fozzie! The Door in a Jar!" yelled Kermit.

Fozzie held up Bunsen's jar. "Here it is!" he said. He started to read the label out loud. "Open jar away from face. Contents may have settled due to shipping. Avoid contact with eyes—"

"Just . . . throw it!" shouted Kermit.

Fozzie threw the jar at the wall in front of them, and it broke open. *Whoosh!*

A very small door magically appeared in the wall. A *very* small door. It was so small, in fact, that only Pepe could fit through it.

Kermit picked up the jar and looked at the tiny

picture of a door on its label. "Hmmm," he said. "Kinda disappointing."

Miss Piggy was more vocal. "Bunsen! I'm gonna kill that melon-headed little poindexter!" she swore.

Meanwhile, Pepe was ducking through the door. "Works for me! Adiós!" he said. The door shut behind him just as Rizzo got to it.

"I can't believe that little shrimp left us behind!" said Rizzo.

Suddenly, a full-size door opened down the hall, and there was Pepe! "Hey. I am not a shrimp, I am a king prawn!" he said, very heroically.

"Let's get outta here!" said Gonzo. They all sprinted for the door Pepe had opened, the guards hot on their heels. Gonzo, bringing up the rear, just managed to slam the door behind him in time.

They were out! But they weren't safe yet.

Two guards stood near the entrance to the building, deep in conversation. Gonzo and his friends tiptoed by behind them, unnoticed.

Just then, the security sirens began to scream. The two guards engaged their weapons and jumped to attention. The Muppets made a break for the bus as the building lit up with searchlights.

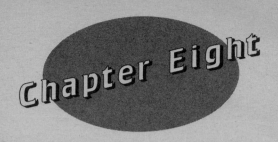

Chapter Eight

*T*he Muppets, safely aboard the bus, cheered. "We did it! We made it!" they shouted.

Gonzo joined in. "That was incredible! Now we can go meet my alien brothers at Cape Doom!"

The cheering stopped. Everyone was silent. They stared at Gonzo in disbelief.

Rizzo spoke first. "Come on, buddy, give it a break."

"What?" Gonzo shouted. "You mean you guys still don't believe me?"

"Uhh...what makes you think that aliens are landing there, Gonzo?" asked Kermit.

"A sandwich told me!" replied Gonzo.

"Gonzo!" yelled his exasperated friends.

"All right. Fine. Stop the bus," Gonzo said. "I'll get there by myself."

"No, Gonzo, wait," said Kermit. "It doesn't matter what we believe. If you believe that you need to go

and meet your alien brothers, then I say...
I say...we're going to the beach!"

The bus was quiet for a moment while everyone thought this over. And then...

"Let's go!" shouted the rest of the Muppets.

Miss Piggy leaned over to talk to Kermit, her cell phone clutched to her chest. "Kermie, that was beautiful," she said. Then she quickly turned her back and resumed talking on the phone.

• • •

Singer and Rentro were in Singer's office when the Covnet security sirens sounded. Singer was sitting in his high-backed chair.

"I hear sirens," he said to himself.

"The alien broke through security and left the premises, sir," reported Rentro.

"We have to find out where he's going," said Singer.

Rentro responded quickly. "Well, I didn't overhear anything."

Singer narrowed his eyes at Rentro. "Did I ask you if you overheard anything?"

"Uh...um...no," said Rentro nervously.

"Because if you had overheard anything, I'm sure you would tell me," said Singer. "Or need I remind you again of Mr. Jumbo's Circus Town and Wild Animal Revue?" he added cruelly.

"No, no, sir!" said Rentro quickly.

"Where is he?" said Singer, hunting around for a Mr. Jumbo brochure. "Oh, look Sunday is half price at the petting zoo." He waved the brochure in Rentro's face. Rentro looked panic-stricken.

"Okay, okay, okay!" said Rentro. "He's headed for Cape Doom!"

Singer nodded. "Good, good. Get me the sub-atomic neutro-destablilizer."

Rentro looked at him blankly.

"The *really big gun!*" Singer explained, rolling his eyes.

Rentro nodded dejectedly. Then he turned and opened a high-tech cabinet. Under a bright, cold light sat a big, futuristic, menacing-looking weapon. Beside it was an ammunition clip with a scary, blinking red light. Rentro gulped as Singer stepped forward to take down the weapon. He locked and loaded the clip. He smiled coldly. "Let's head to my car," he said.

"Uh, problem there. You remember those parking tickets you asked me to take care of? Well, uh—your car's impounded. We can take the company car."

• • •

In the Electric Mayhem bus, Miss Piggy was speaking into her cell phone in a whisper. "Mikey, get the crew down to Cape Doom on the double! And this is my exclusive, so don't tell anyone!"

She hung up.

Kermit and the gang may not have been at the Muppet boarding house, but the Muppet boarding house was not deserted. Just the opposite: It was a zoo. Quite a crowd had gathered—the whole front yard was full of Gonzo's devoted followers, wearing fake Gonzo noses. There were also Muppets, neighbors, and the "UFO Mania" news crew. Mikey, the cameraman, had just gotten off his cell phone with Miss Piggy. "Pack it up, guys!" he yelled loudly to his crew. "*The spaceship's landing at Cape Doom!*"

Everybody heard him—Gonzo's followers, Muppets, neighbors, the whole crowd. They immediately began to stampede in the direction of Cape Doom.

• • •

A cement truck lumbered down the road at ten miles per hour, its engine whining in protest. Cars passed it, honking. Singer and Rentro sat inside. *This* was the company car.

"Can't this thing go any faster?" Singer said impatiently.

"Safety first, sir," replied Rentro.

• • •

When the Electric Mayhem bus got to Cape Doom, the beach was crawling with people. Everybody

71

who'd been at the Muppet boarding house had gotten there first.

Kermit gave Miss Piggy an accusing look.

She shrugged. "Can I help it if moi has such a devoted following?" she said.

The bus pulled to a stop at the entrance to the beach. Instantly, the bus was thronged by people trying to get to Gonzo. They waved signs celebrating Gonzo and welcoming the aliens.

"Gon-zo! Gon-zo! Gon-zo!" they chanted.

"Wow!" said Gonzo, looking around in amazement as he got off the bus.

Somebody shoved a megaphone into Gonzo's face.

"Say something," whispered Rizzo.

Gonzo got up close to the megaphone. "Uh…hi," he said uncertainly. The crowd went wild.

Gonzo and the Muppets began to make their way through the crowd and down to the beach. There were not only believers there, but also people who had set up stands to sell alien-related souvenirs. It was hard to move through the mass of people.

"We need to get to the beach," said Gonzo urgently.

"Let me handle this," said Rizzo. He yelled to the crowd at the top of his lungs. "All right, everybody, back off! Make way for the alien! Make way for His Royal Weirdness!"

"Looks like you have a lot of believers," Kermit said to Gonzo.

"Looks like you have a lot of bozos," said Miss Piggy.

As Gonzo walked through the crowd, some of the Gonzomaniacs reached out and touched him. Others took his picture. Farther down the beach, some of them had built bonfires and were dancing around them.

"This is some wacky clambake, okay?" said Pepe.

Suddenly—eek!—Rizzo ran straight into Dr. Phil Van Neuter! Rizzo gasped and backed away in horror.

"It's okay, Rizzo," said a familiar voice. Rizzo looked around to find Bubba and all the other lab rats. They were hanging out with Dr. Phil!

"We let him slide and he gave us a ride," Bubba explained to Rizzo.

"Bubba," said Rizzo, "I never got a chance to thank you for what you guys did."

"Hey, you led the break, man. You did for us, we did for you."

"Yeah, that's the Rat's Credo!" said one of the other lab rats.

"I thought the Rat's Credo was 'There's garbage. Let's eat!'" said Rizzo.

"Garbage? Where?" said another rat.

"Over there! Let's eat!" And they scurried off, leaving Dr. Phil behind, happily dancing the limbo.

By nightfall, the party was still going on. The beach was packed with people waiting for the aliens to arrive at midnight. It was time for Miss Piggy to do her TV report. She smoothed her dress, took a deep breath, and began. This was her moment of triumph.

"Hello, everyone! This is Miss Piggy with a 'UFO Mania' exclusive: 'Alien Gonzo, the Final Chapter.'"

"You! I don't believe this!" interrupted a voice. Miss Piggy turned to see who would dare break in on her big news story.

It was Shelley Snipes, the regular "UFO Mania" anchorwoman. Her hands were on her hips. She was angry. Very angry, in fact.

"Shelley! Hello!" said Miss Piggy, nonchalantly.

"You backstabbing, underhanded little . . . coffee pig!" she spat. "This is *my* show and *my* story. Give me that microphone!"

Shelley made a grab for the microphone, but Miss Piggy wasn't going to let it go. Shelley pulled. Miss Piggy pulled. They got into a regular tug-of-war, right there on live television.

Miss Piggy turned to the camera with as sweet a smile as she could manage. "If my fans will excuse moi for a moment," she said. Then she turned back to Shelley. "*Hiiiiii-ya!*" she screamed as she flipped Shelley to the ground. The struggle continued until Miss Piggy brought out her secret weapon: the spray bottle full of Muppet Labs Mind Mist. She gave Shelley a good spritz, right in the face.

Suddenly Shelley looked confused. "What. . .what was I doing?" she said.

"Uh…you were just going to give me your job and devote your career to helping me," Miss Piggy explained.

"Oh! That's right. Is there anything you need, Miss Piggy?"

Miss Piggy thought fast. "Um, yes. A cup of coffee, please."

"Coming right up," said Shelley, stumbling off in a daze.

In the distance, a clock tower could be heard striking twelve. Miss Piggy went right back into her broadcast without missing a beat. "Midnight!" she said dramatically. "The lone alien stands before a naked sky. The mood is tense. My hair looks great."

Everyone watched and waited. The time had come.

Chapter Nine

An hour later, the sky was still empty. Up and down the beach, the bonfires were burning low.

"One A.M.," reported Miss Piggy. "The alien is still standing here. My hair still looks great. One can only wonder what Gonzo is feeling right now…."

"They're not coming," said Gonzo sadly.

"Maybe they're just running late," said Kermit.

"It's a no-show," said Gonzo. He chuckled to himself. "Ha! A no-show." He began to laugh hysterically.

The crowd started to stir. They were angry and disappointed.

"I believed you, man!" someone shouted. People started throwing their Gonzo signs into the garbage.

"Yeah," said another, coming forward to confront him. "I stayed up all night dancing and didn't study for finals because of you. You lied."

"I feel stupid!" said another.

"I'm cold!" said someone else.

The crowd started to leave the beach. Gonzo didn't know what to say. Somebody threw a fake Gonzo nose at him. Kermit tried to comfort him, but Gonzo was destroyed.

They didn't notice a little girl in the crowd, being led off by her mother. She dragged her feet, turning to take one last look up at the sky. And as she did, her face lit up in wonder. She stopped and pointed.

"Look!" she said.

A couple of people looked up. Then all over the beach, people were starting to point upward.

A globe-shaped spacecraft was zigzagging across the sky.

It was moving very fast. The crowd gasped—the ship was heading straight for them! It was landing, right in their midst! It was…it was…

Eighteen inches across?

It plopped into the sand, nestled down, and just sat there. After some hesitation, the crowd approached it cautiously, forming a circle around the craft.

"Gee," said Gonzo, leaning in for a closer look. "They're a little smaller than I thought . . ."

Suddenly, the little round spaceship moved. It was opening! Four petal-like parts began to unfold, making it look like some kind of space flower. As the surprised crowd backed away, an incredibly bright beam of light flooded out from inside the ship.

And then people began pointing up again. The little round ship was just the beginning. Hovering just a few feet over their heads was a *huge* spaceship! This one was magnificent! The crowd gaped in awe.

"The little blue freak was right!" Miss Piggy said in amazement.

"Holy moley!" said Pepe.

Rizzo dropped to his knees. "Please, Big Boss, I always obeyed my mother, and I never carried the plague, not even once!"

The ship touched down on the beach, and the crowd watched as the smoke slowly cleared. Mysterious and saucerlike, the ship was bathed in shifting iridescent colored lights. It was beautiful.

"How are you feeling?" Kermit asked Gonzo.

"Great. Never felt better," said a terrified Gonzo.

"Don't worry, you'll be fine," said Kermit.

Just then, the spaceship door began to open.

"*Yahhhhhh!*" screamed Kermit and Gonzo together.

From the blinding light of the ship's open doorway, a ramp emerged and touched down on the sand. Then a dark figure appeared at the doorway. It was hard to see the figure clearly, because the light behind it was so bright.

The mysterious figure spoke. "*Let the one who is called Gonzo step forward,*" it said.

Gonzo stepped forward. "That's me," he said nervously. "I'm Gonzo!"

"*Step a little closer*," said the figure.

Gonzo approached the ship, shaking like a leaf.

"*Can you lean into the light?*" said the voice.

At the same time, the figure leaned forward himself to get a better look at Gonzo. "*Yep! It's him!*" the figure said finally.

The figure moved back into the ship. The crowd was silent. What would happen now?

Suddenly the top of the ship separated from the bottom, lifting into the air to reveal a spectacular performance stage.

"Whoa!" said Gonzo.

And then, a spotlight hit center stage, revealing the mysterious figure and bathing him in light. Now everyone could see he was neither large nor menacing. In fact, he looked a lot like Gonzo. He seemed to be acting as a sort of master of ceremonies, a leader...an UberGonzo.

"Gonzo," he said, "many zotons ago, you were lost to us. Since then, we have been searching, looking high and low. We've come a long way looking for you, little brother."

As he spoke, dozens of Gonzo-like creatures emerged from the smoke and light, and lined up on the edge of the stage.

Miss Piggy stared. "As if one of them wasn't enough."

"We have missed you," continued the UberGonzo.

"Today is a good day. It's a reunion for all of us."

Suddenly spectacular fireworks and laser effects erupted onstage. Then the stage went black.

It was time for the big show. Music! Glitter! Dancing and singing! Amazing unicycle and trampoline tricks! The crowd went wild, loving every minute of the incredible show.

And for the grand finale, Gonzo was brought up on stage. The UberGonzo handed him a shiny helmet. Then, amid great fanfare, Gonzo was stuffed into a cannon. The crowd held their breath as an alien lit the fuse with a fiery sparkler.

"Good luck, Gonzo!" said the UberGonzo.

It was all so very familiar to Gonzo. "Oh my gosh," he said. "I remember!"

Kaboom! went the cannon. Gonzo blasted out, soaring up, up, up into the starry sky. He hung, suspended for a moment, then began to plummet back down to Earth.

"Now who went and put too much gunpowder in the cannon again?" asked the UberGonzo.

"*Ahhhhhhhh!*" screamed Gonzo. Two of the Gonzos rushed around the stage holding a paper hoop, trying to determine exactly where Gonzo would land.

Suddenly—*splat!* Gonzo tore right through the hoop and the stage. The crowd gasped. Where was Gonzo?

The crowd screamed with delight as he appeared, his arms triumphantly aloft. "Gonzo! Gonzo! Gonzo!" they chanted.

• • •

Meanwhile, out in the parking lot, the cement truck pulled up next to the Electric Mayhem bus.

"That wasn't so bad," said Rentro.

"Out!" yelled Singer.

• • •

Down on the beach, the Gonzos and the Muppets were mingling. Fozzie had seized the opportunity to try out his jokes on a new audience.

"Knock, knock," he began. The Gonzos instantly cracked up in hysterics. "Good crowd!" said Fozzie.

The UberGonzo, meanwhile, was introducing Gonzo to the aliens. "…And over there is Oznog," he said, "and that's Nozgo and Zogno, and over there is—well, I'll let them introduce themselves."

"This is so amazing," said Gonzo in awe.

"Our show just hasn't been the same without Gonzo the Cannonball. It is many queelinks that we have been searching for you."

"Queelinks? What's a queelink?" said Gonzo.

"About a hundred farnoks," explained the UberGonzo.

"Oh," said Gonzo.

"It's time we departed," said the UberGonzo. "We have a gig on Alpha Centuri, and the asteroid belt is murder at rush hour."

"You mean, go?" said Gonzo. "Now?"

"As we say on planet Goznog, 'The show must get down!'"

"Oh. Well—this is all happening so fast," said Gonzo. "Uh…"

He faced his friends. Gonzo was having difficulty finding the right words. "Gee, there are so many things I want to say to each of you. I don't know where to start! I know I'll miss you, and I'll be thinking of you. You guys really came through for me."

He looked at Fozzie. "Hey, Fozzie—" he began.

"Wait," said Fozzie, "do you know the secret to playing golf in outer space?"

"No, what?"

"A black hole in one! Ah*aaa*…aaahhaaa." Fozzie was bravely trying to laugh, but could not keep his laughter from turning into tears.

Gonzo turned to Miss Piggy, who motioned her camera crew over in order to milk the dramatic moment. "Get this, get this," she hissed at them.

"Piggy, there's something I want to tell you…" said Gonzo.

"Yes?" said Miss Piggy.

Gonzo threw his arms around her. "I've always had

a crush on you!" he confessed.

Miss Piggy pushed him away. "Yecch! Cut!" she said to the cameraman.

Gonzo walked over to Rizzo next.

"Oh no. Not me," said Rizzo. "I don't do good-byes."

"Rizzo, I want you to take care of yourself."

Rizzo choked back tears. "Don't worry about me. I'll find another roommate. It's easy for a rat to find a roommate." He broke down crying, and Gonzo hugged him.

Then it was Kermit's turn. "And Kermit? Well, you're the best friend any alien could ask for," said Gonzo.

"Well, I love you, Gonzo." They hugged. "Promise you'll write."

"Sure, I will. There's probably a mailbox every couple of farnoks." They both laughed tearfully.

Now Clifford and Pepe ambled up to Gonzo. "Okay, okay, okay, okay. Good-bye spaceman, okay?" said Pepe, tired of this teary scene.

"Yeah, man," added Clifford. "You keep sayin' good-bye, you'll never get home."

"Yeah," said Gonzo thoughtfully. "Home." He took a deep breath and gathered his determination. "Time to go home."

Chapter Ten

Suddenly there was a commotion at the edge of the crowd. It was Singer, disguised as a Gonzomaniac in a fake Gonzo nose and Gonzo T-shirt. In his arms he held the huge subatomic neutro-destabilizer. As the crowd backed away fearfully, he stepped toward Gonzo.

"Very moving, my alien friend," he said, "but your timing is a little off."

"Mr. Singer," said Gonzo pleadingly.

Singer stepped closer. "So you really think you were going to just disappear without a trace. Oh, that must be fun for you to play that little game. Well, guess what? This game is over, and I win. And winner takes all, baby! Now you're all coming back with me...in my cement truck!"

He was distracted by the sound of giggling nearby. "Who's laughing?" he demanded to know. "What's so funny? Don't laugh at me!"

As the giggling continued, Singer realized it was coming from the Alien Gonzos. They found him very amusing.

"All right, you little . . . things! I'll show you funny!" Singer swung around with the weapon and pointed it at the Alien Gonzos.

"No, wait!" Gonzo hurled himself between the gun and the Alien Gonzos.

Everyone watched in horror.

"*Noooo!!!*" wailed Rizzo.

Singer pulled the trigger.

Click! There was a female digital voice. "Please load weapon," it said.

Singer, furious, pulled the trigger a few more times, but nothing happened. The crowd sighed in relief.

"No, this isn't happening!" screamed Singer. "No!" He threw the weapon on the ground and stomped up and down on the gun in a rage. Then he stopped jumping and kicked it, stubbing his toe on the heavy gun. He hopped around on one foot, screaming, "Ow! Ow! My toe!"

The Alien Gonzos laughed even harder at Singer. And their laughter was contagious. Pretty soon, everyone else was laughing too.

"Whew!" said Kermit to Rentro, who was standing beside him. "That was close."

"Well, not that close, my friend." Rentro chuckled.

He held up the ammunition clip from the subatomic neutro-destabilizer, with its small blinking red light. Kermit laughed.

Singer, still hopping on one foot, accidentally slipped on the gun and went flying with a shriek. Next to the spaceship, the UberGonzo turned to Oznog, impressed. "This Earthling is gooood," he said.

Finally, Singer rose, exhausted and defeated, his face covered in sand. He spit out a mouthful of sand and started to sob. The UberGonzo approached him. "We are honored to meet you," said the alien.

"A most extraordinary performance," added Oznog.

"What are you *talking* about?" wailed Singer.

"Gonzo of Earth. Who is this most entertaining human friend of yours?" inquired the UberGonzo. "He must be revered as a king on your planet."

"That's Mr. Singer. Yes, he's a real card," said Gonzo.

"Mr. Singer," said the UberGonzo enthusiastically, "we must have you as a guest performer. The galaxy cannot be denied your talents!"

"Yeah! That's right. Big talent!" agreed the other Alien Gonzos.

"You mean, you want me to go with you?" asked the amazed Singer.

The UberGonzo helped Singer up by the arm as the other Alien Gonzos gathered around. "It would be our great privilege, Mr. Singer. May I call you…Zongo?"

"To boldly go where no man has gone before? To travel the stars like a modern-day Magellan? I'll do it!"

"Excellent!" said the UberGonzo. "This way, Zongo."

As they headed up the ramp to the ship, Gonzo looked back at his friends. He seemed to be deep in thought.

"The stars beckon!" the UberGonzo called to Gonzo. "Shall we go home?"

"No," said Gonzo. "I don't think so." He removed his helmet and handed it to the UberGonzo. "I'm sorry. I just can't leave. I'm just finally realizing that, although I'm related to you guys, and I'm really glad I met you"—he turned to Kermit and the others— "…these guys are my family, and this is my home," he finished.

He walked down the ramp again to join his friends.

"If that is your decision, then we shall abide by it," said the UberGonzo to Gonzo. "Good luck, Gonzo!" Then the alien leader addressed the crowd. "People of Earth! Later!" he said.

As they continued up the ramp to the ship, the UberGonzo leaned over to Singer. "Oh, by the way," he said, "have you ever been shot out of a cannon?"

Singer looked confused. "What? Oh, you're joking! Ha-ha. You are kidding, right?" The ship's door shut.

Then, as Gonzo and the rest of the crowd watched,

the spaceship lifted off and disappeared into the twinkling cosmos.

• • •

Later that night, under that same twinkling blanket of stars, Gonzo sat on the roof of the Muppet boarding house with his friends.

"What a great day," he said. "That was probably the best day of my whole life. There's just one thing I still don't understand." His nose glowed in the moon-light.

"What's that, Gonzo?" asked Kermit.

"Why did they ask me to build a Jacuzzi?"

It was quiet on the roof. No one wanted to break the news to Gonzo.

"You know," Rizzo said at last, "that is the beauty of life. The little unanswered questions, the mysterious mysteries."

"He's right, okay?" Pepe added quickly. "Listen to him, he makes good sense."

"Why is the sky blue?" said Rizzo, waxing even more philosophical. "Why are we all sitting on the roof? Sometimes you just have to say, 'I may never know, and that's…okay.'"

Gonzo thought for a moment. "Gee, Rizzo. That's really beautiful," he said.